Bring Me the Head of Philip K. Dick's Simulacrum

Kendall Evans

Bring Me the Head of Philip K. Dick's Simulacrum
by Kendall Evans

Story copyright owned by Kendall Evans
Cover art "Robotic Delirium" by Sandy DeLuca
Cover design by Laura Givens

First Printing July 2018

Hiraeth Publishing
P.O. Box 1248
Tularosa, NM 88352
e-mail: sdpshowcase@yahoo.com

Visit www.hiraethsffh.com for online science fiction, fantasy, horror, scifaiku, and more. Stop by our online Shop for novels, magazines, anthologies, and collections. **Support the small, independent press...and your First Amendment rights.**

Bring Me the Head of Philip K. Dick's Simulacrum

Flicker of fire in the window

At the periphery of vision. But when he turned his head sharply there was nothing there; not even reflected light to explain the misperception.

Incendiary dreams last night. Maybe this was a leftover. In the dream he had been trapped in a building, lost in a maze of shifting, smoke-obscured licks of flame. He dreamed he was slapping at burning clothing, and evidently, he had actually slapped himself; the motion startled him awake. A serial nightmare. The same dream, with slight variations, three or four times of late.

Shoving memories of the dream aside, he concentrated on invoicing his clients, readying the bills with the intention of posting them in the afternoon's mail: two cases completed, one satisfactorily, the other not-so-much-so. Infidelity easily proven photographically in the first instance, but the second case remained unresolved, the missing person still missing, all his leads dead-ending.

Paperwork was his nemesis, but the invoicing helped keep him from wondering where his next client would come from. Back when he was on the force, he had finished his reports promptly because he had no choice. Now he tended to procrastinate.

The knock on his office door was a welcome distraction.

3

He ushered in a young woman in her late twenties – his best estimate – casually dressed, her brunette hair bobbed short.

"Are you Brandon Andrade?"

Yes. Please call me Brad. And you are?"

"Isis."

"Isis?" he said, the questioning tone his way of asking for her last name.

"Isis is sufficient."

"Have a seat. Please."

She wore distressed Levis, faded blue, with partial holes above the knees and stripes of tanned leg showing between frayed white cross-strands. She did not bother to remove the dark glasses concealing her eyes. The halter top allowed him an attractive view of her flat, sun-tanned abdomen and ring-pierced navel.

"What can I do for you?"

"We want you to bring us the head of Philip K. Dick's simulacrum."

"Bring you the what, *what*?" he asked, sensing the conversation was getting ahead of him. "Bring you a simulacrum?" Was that the hint of a smile? She must have realized her request would puzzle him; she might as well have asked him to secure a magic speculum.

"Maybe it would be better to describe it as an android head, or the head of a robot. No, wait a minute. You've seen that old Abraham Lincoln attraction at Disneyland, haven't you? The audio-animatronics figure?"

He nodded agreement.

"And you've heard of Philip K. Dick?"

"Isn't he a science fiction writer? Didn't he write *Blade Runner*?

"Yes. No." She shook her head. "He wrote a novel titled *Do Androids Dream of Electric Sheep.*

4

The movie *Blade Runner* was supposedly based on the novel, but the two were really quite different. Personally, I prefer the novel." There was something nearly British in her diction, but no trace of an accent.

"Do I detect prejudice?" He wondered if she was a fan of the author, or perhaps some sort of agent; wondered, too, if she had the resources to finance an investigation.

She smoothed her dark hair and gave him a knowing look. "This is business, Mr. Andrade. Philip Dick died in March of 1982. After his death, Hanson Robotics created a robot in the likeness of the author. It was one of the most advanced of its time, programmed to respond to questions and capable of quoting lengthily from the author's works. A fairly sophisticated artificial intelligence."

"But not truly intelligent or conscious," he interrupted, revising his age estimate to early thirties. Though not beautiful, she was attractive, with a sensuous attitude difficult to pin down.

"No," she admitted. "It wouldn't pass a Turing Test. Many of its responses seemed random or non sequitur. It tended to make statements or offer quotations totally out of context. But it was extremely sophisticated and well-received at the NextFest Fair; one of the most popular exhibits at the event.

"Later on, David Hanson was transporting the robot on a flight from Dallas to San Francisco for another demonstration. But there was a stopover in Las Vegas and an unexpected flight change; he forgot about the android's head for a moment and left it in an overhead luggage compartment. It hasn't been seen since."

"How long ago was the flight?" he asked.

"Nearly six months."

"It's an old trail," He said. "Pretty much a cold case. Why did you wait so long to contact me?"

For a moment he stared out the window with its disheartening view of the brick building opposite, but his thoughts were elsewhere. Ever since reality had become problematical, some four or five years ago, he frequently suffered vivid dreams, most of them nightmarish.

He wondered whether today's reality index was low; he hadn't had a chance to check the newspaper yet.

"Sorry," he said, realizing she had been talking while his mind wandered. "I missed that. Something about another investigator?"

"Yes, but let me back up a little. At first American West said they had located the American Tourister bag containing the head – a black bag, appropriately enough – and were forwarding it to San Francisco, but it never arrived. Later they said it must be somewhere in their unclaimed luggage department and it would surely turn up. Before long, their reassurances seemed more like platitudes. After two months with no results, we hired a private investigator from a Las Vegas firm. He failed to accomplish anything worthwhile. This is a copy of his report."

Her purse was large enough to accommodate the letter-sized manila file folder that she passed across to Brad. He placed it on his desk.

Once more she searched her purse. "You'll need this," she said. "It's a video tape of some conversations with the android. It will help you recognize the head if you find it." She handed across a VHS tape, followed by several paperback books. "You should also read these."

He studied the covers for a moment: *The Man in the High Castle, Do Androids Dream of Electric Sheep,* and *Eye in the Sky* . . . all three novels by the late author. Her damn purse must be a virtual cornucopia.

"Seriously?" he said. "Do you really think reading some of his novels will help with my investigations?"

Pausing a moment, she looked thoughtful. "Yes. Oddly enough, I think it will. At least it will give you some idea of what you're involved in. I think you should also get a copy of *We Can Build You.* I didn't have an extra one handy." Though skeptical, he did not ask how the author's fictional efforts could have anything to do with events that had taken place after his death.

"Why did you choose me?" he asked.

"We went to the L.A.P.D. The officer I spoke with recommended you. He said you were stubborn. Persistent, I think he said."

He rubbed at his beard; realized it needed trimming. "Once upon a time I worked for the L.A.P.D. I still have a few friends there."

"Will you take the case?"

"I don't want to offer any false hope. . ." He scanned the folder's contents while she waited. "But I'm confident I can be more thorough than the previous detective. And, yes, I'll take the case." He didn't have much choice, considering the state of his current finances. "Four hundred a day plus expenses . . . is that satisfactory? And I'll need a retainer, say twelve hundred, to get me started."

She surprised him by paying with cash, and provided a contact phone number, but no card bearing either a company or personal name. "We prefer to remain anonymous. Also, there's a twenty-five-hundred-dollar reward. If you're successful, you'll have that plus your fee."

For the next few minutes he asked pointed questions; took notes.

Watching her departure, he lingered in the doorway, enjoying the view of her backside as she strode toward the elevators. *Isis?* Somehow, he doubted it was her real name.

* * * * *

Minutes later, unfolding the front page of today's *Los Angeles Times*, dated June 17, 1987, he immediately sought the day's reality index. The familiar rectangle was there, located as always on the lower half of the front page. The words within the box, in bold 28-point type, read:

TODAY'S REALITY INDEX: 78%

Perhaps the low figure helped to explain the bizarre case of the missing android's head that had fallen into his hands. He, like many, used the index as a forecast for whether he should expect unlikely difficulties to come his way, or absurdities perhaps best ignored. Normally the index averaged in the low to mid-nineties, but of late it had been nearly as erratic as the stock market.

Today's figure was only a couple of points higher than the all-time low. In November of the previous year it had dipped to a stunning seventy-six percent. Record numbers of people had called in sick or taken vacation time, unwilling to venture forth from the supposed safety of their own homes, fearful of what might occur at that level of uncertainty.

Not long ago he had read an article about how the stats were derived. Cooperating scientists from numerous disciplines computed a wide range of factors daily, including neutrino behavior, extreme weather events, inappropriate atomic decay, aberrant wave-patterns generated in double-slit experiments, interstellar anomalies reported by astronomers, and sociological considerations such as work-place shootings, to generate their figures. There had been a number of other factors, but he could not recall all of them. Most experts agreed, claiming the first perturbations of reality had actually occurred five years ago. However, it wasn't until well over two years later that the theory became widely accepted, and the daily index box began appearing in newspapers.

Of course, there were naysayers – those who claimed the index was nonsensical, and merely a reflection of society's current paranoia. Brad tried to keep an open mind on the subject; yet he continued to check the index every day, almost religiously, knowing it impacted his attitude.

None of the headlines in the newspaper struck him as particularly interesting or important, so he opened the file folder and skimmed through the information Isis had provided.

Several pages were stapled together: the previous investigator's report, on a letterhead which read "Iverson Inquiries", with a Las Vegas address. The actual investigator was named Albert Poulson, and as Brad suspected, his efforts had been little more than cursory – a plus, from his standpoint.

Poulson had interviewed David Hanson, the man transporting the head when it was lost; a stewardess or flight attendant named Stevie Nicholson; Alice Evans, a P.R. representative for the airline; and Robert Simms in the lost luggage / baggage claims department. He had failed to contact any passengers on the flight. *Not at all thorough, he decided.* Excepting a visit to the Las Vegas and San Francisco Lost Luggage Departments, all of Poulson's interviews had been by phone. In person was always best.

The mail arrived, forced through the slot in his door by the postman and spilling to the floor. He stooped to retrieve it, sorting the envelopes. He dropped the junk-mail into the trash and placed three new bills in his inbox. There was also an Off-Road Revelers newsletter. He was a long-time member. He opened it and noticed a Northern California trip planned in August by his fellow members, and decided to sign up for it, caseload permitting.

He returned his attention to the file for the new case. *Where to begin?* He narrowed down the possibilities and considered calling the other detective – but what motive would there be for helping belatedly close the case? A resolution now could make the initial investigation look shoddy.

Start with the stewardess, he decided. *She's my best bet, at least for now.*

Fortunately, the previous detective, Poulson, had been thorough enough to provide contact information for everyone he interviewed. He copied Stevie Nicholson's name, Dallas address and phone number into his notebook, and immediately dialed her number. No answer; he had to content himself with leaving a message.

He wanted to see the tape of the android as soon as possible, but there was no VHS player in his office; only the one in his apartment. He decided to leave early. The invoicing could wait until tomorrow.

* * * * *

On the flight to Dallas, he leaned back and closed his eyes. He wanted to stretch out his legs too, but there wasn't enough room, so he made do.

That VHS tape of the android. *Uncanny.* He had watched it after leaving his office on Wednesday. Never before had he seen such a convincing simulation of a human being's facial expressions, eye and eyebrow movements, and conversation. He had watched it three times, all the way through. The android, seated in a chair, dressed – he had read – in the late author's clothing, conversing with several different people. The damn thing even blinked its eyes in what seemed a randomly natural way.

Seeing the video had been advantageous. An image of Dick's android head loomed in his mind like a trophy. He wanted to find it. Accomplish what others had failed to do.

He also still hoped to find the missing college student, Christina Diego. Even though he had theoretically closed the case, he still had feelers out. He had not given up on discovering her location.

After watching the tape, he started reading *Do Androids Dream of Electric Sheep*, and he had not been able to stop. In the early a.m. hours, he finished reading the novel in one night. Finally, he had grabbed a few hours of sleep, knowing that he would again arrive late at his office.

Airline flights always reminded him of the frailty of human flesh. Today's takeoff had been no exception: that vibrating rush along the runway, the anticipatory surge of adrenalin. . .

Brad had wanted to interview the stewardess as soon as possible, hopefully in L.A. or Las Vegas, but she had been reassigned to flights going east. And she wouldn't be available to talk with him until today, Monday. Soon after she called back he booked his flight and finally forced himself to take care of sending out invoices and paying bills.

The flight to Dallas was early, so his window seat did not afford much of a view. When the dark-eyed stewardess made her rounds, he ordered a gin and tonic, continuing to mull over the past few days.

Due to the delay in his case, he had decided to visit his daughter. As arranged by phone the night before, he drove down to San Diego on Friday, and picked Savannah up from the neighbor's house where she stayed while his ex-wife Gladys was working at the DMV. After the divorce, Gladys had insisted on moving to San Diego, and he felt he was losing touch with his daughter. He and Savannah spent the day at Sea World. It wasn't as much of a disaster as he feared; still, he remembered sitting waiting for the Killer Whale show, and turning his head to study his nine-year-old daughter. Their conversations together had flagged. He could sense the growing distance between them. Was she bored? The love that he felt for her seemed to collide with an impenetrable barrier; her emotional shield? His uncertainty? When a park employee came around selling brilliant blue beach towels, patterned with leaping dolphins, he bought three as a token gesture: one for Savannah, one for Gladys, and one for himself.

"If you go to the beach this summer, you and your Mom will have matching beach towels. And mine will always remind me of you." He wanted her to respond to his words. Her silence stung.

His right leg felt cramped and half-asleep; annoying little pinpricks of sensation. He stared out the jet airliner's double-paned window, jiggling both legs up and down to improve circulation.

After dropping his daughter off with Gladys, he had driven home the same evening, arriving late at his apartment. Keyed up, nearly overwhelmed with regrets and knowing that he could not sleep, he spent the night reading *The Man in the High Castle*. The novel was an alternate history, bizarre, yet lucid and well written. The premise, the idea that the Axis Powers had won World War II, was intricately developed. According to the back-cover blurb, the book had won something called the Hugo award for best SF novel of the year.

For years he had enjoyed reading authors like Ross MacDonald, Raymond Chandler, and Joseph Wambaugh's police procedurals; but none of them got under his skin like Dick did. He had already completed reading all three of the books that Isis provided. Otherwise, he would be reading now, on the flight.

Drink unfinished, he dozed off. While the passenger jet descended toward the Dallas-Fort Worth Airport, he dreamed that flames danced all around.

* * * * *

Stevie Nicholson lived in a duplex condominium surrounded by a landscaped, gated community in Dallas. A concrete walk wound its way around natural-looking, glacial-sized rocks and an artificial stream. He crossed two bridges, glimpsing colorful koi in pooled blue water, before reaching her door.

The stewardess answered her doorbell wearing a modest robe, a moist terrycloth towel wrapping her head. His fault -- he compulsively arrived early for pre-arranged appointments.

"Hi," Brad said. "Sorry I'm early. If this is inconvenient, I can come back later."

"That's o.k. Come on in. I'll introduce you to Richard."

Over the phone she had warned him that she was taking care of her nephew for a couple of days. "He's impaired," she had explained. "He's been diagnosed with everything from PDD to autism and Childhood Onset Schizophrenia, depending on which doctor you talk to. He gets to be too much for my sister sometimes. Poor Julie – she needs a break once in a while. He can be a real handful."

In the living room, austere-modern, she invited him to take a seat.

"This is Richard," she said. "He just turned twelve last month. Richard, this is Brandon Andrade. He's a private detective."

Children his age were often impressed to meet a real-life private detective, but Richard accepted it stoically, giving no response at all.

His gaze shifted from some far horizon to nearby objects not present in his aunt's living room. The boy had not looked at him directly since he entered.

"Hi, Richard. You can call me Brad." Stevie Nicholson excused herself and disappeared down a hallway.

"Hi," Richard said. At least he had responded. "Did Aunt Stevie tell you about me?"

"Yes. She said you were visiting with her."

One of Richard's arms was wrapped in a plaster cast. He was freckle-faced and spindle thin; pale and fragile-looking.

"Did she tell you I can see the future?"

"Yes. She did mention that. I think she said, specifically, that you can see the year 2014."

"She's wrong, you know," the boy informed him, voice nearly toneless and matter-of-fact. He was so soft spoken that Brad leaned forward to better hear his words.

"She's wrong? How's that?"

"I *can't* see the future. This really is the year 2014, not 1987."

His curiosity went into overdrive. "How can that be?"

"I'm not certain," he said. "Some sort of cosmic sleight-of-hand. I keep trying to figure it out, but maybe I never will." Schizophrenic he might be, but he was unusually articulate for a twelve-year-old.

"Let me get this straight. When you look around, you can actually see events taking place in 2014? People and objects that your aunt and I can't see?"

"Of course." The persistent drone of what he assumed must be a hairdryer sounded from deeper in the condo.

15

"What about me? Can you see me, too?"

For the first time, his eyes met Brad's. "Yes, I can see you and hear you, but you're like a ghost. I can see right through you, into the present."

Still jetlagged from his flight, and late hours spent reading, he wanted a cup of coffee. He hoped Stevie Nicholson would offer him some.

"By the present, you mean the year 2014?"

"I already told you that. But there's more to it. The world you see – the world you believe to be 1987 – isn't the real 1987. For instance, do you watch the reality forecast on T.V.?"

"I check the newspaper every morning for the reality index. The percentage figure. I don't watch much television. Why do you ask?"

Richard wrapped his free hand over the cast and rubbed at it, leaning forward. He seemed more interested now, perhaps because Brad was an attentive listener and had not scoffed at his words or argued against his strange assertions.

Initially he had thought the child might be putting him on a bit; testing him with these absurdities. Yet he felt certain, now, that he was face-to-face with delusional convictions, not made-up stories or lies.

In his own way, Richard was genuine.

And he expressed himself with an intelligent lucidity beyond that of many adults – yet with coldly flattened affect.

"Because," he said, "there were no reality indexes in the media in the *real* 1987. No one ever heard of such a thing. As far as I can tell, something happened in 1982 that skewed everything."

"You can see me. You can see this 1987. So how do you know what the real 1987 is like?"

16

"Because I can see that too. Remember it."

His head was spinning, trying to fit the boy's ideas together logically. Though he was intrigued, he longed for the stewardess to return and rescue him from the conversation. He changed the subject, not wanting to press the boy too hard. "How did you break your arm?"

"I was on a stairway in your time; up near the top, climbing down, when I got distracted by a rabbit in real time, and I fell."

"You saw a rabbit. In 2014?"

"Of course. A man and a woman brought in some animals to show the residents. A sort of small traveling petting zoo. I was petting the rabbit when I tripped on the stairs and landed wrong."

"Did the rabbit get hurt too?" he asked, knowing the question ridiculous, but wanting to see how Richard would respond.

"Are you teasing me? The rabbit was safe in my lap in 2014. I was sitting down, rubbing its fur."

"You said you're a resident somewhere in 2014. Are you a patient?"

"My . . . what you would call my condition . . . worsened. I'm kept in a facility. No one pays much attention to me anymore. My Mom's dead by now. Aunt Stevie comes to see me sometimes, but she's old, and all wrinkled. It's so difficult, trying to deal with all these different times at once."

He sounded sad when he said this; his first show of emotion since the two had been introduced.

The real Stevie Nicholson had reentered the room while he was talking, anything but old and wrinkled. The towel was gone, replaced by lush blonde hair trimmed short. She had changed into her uniform and carried a stewardess's cap in one hand. "I think I explained on the phone that I don't have much time. I have a flight this evening, and I need to drop Richard back home before I leave. You two seem to be getting along famously." She seated herself on the sofa next to Richard and gripped his good arm affectionately, her tan brown hand contrasting with Richard's chalky white flesh.

"He was just telling me about the future. Tell me something that hasn't happened yet in my time, Richard. Something that I don't know about – can't know about yet."

"Umm--" Richard said, and then fell silent for a moment. "A few years ago, a politician got shot in the head. A U.S. Representative named Giffords."

"Assassinated? He's dead?"

"She. A woman, not a man. But she didn't die. She's still recovering, I think. Lots of therapy, because it was a brain injury. Her husband was one of the astronauts, but he's retired now."

"I've never heard of her," Brad admitted.

"She'd be too young, wouldn't she? I don't know when she got elected—"

"I don't have much time, Mr. Andrade. You said you have some questions?"

"Of course," he said, embarrassed that she needed to remind him. Normally he was much more focused, zeroing in on getting results. He had allowed himself to become too engrossed in the boy's tapestry of madness. "I'm sorry. Do you recall your interview with Albert Poulson, the investigator who handled the case before I got involved?"

"Yes."

"Have you thought of anything since then that might be of help?"

She looked thoughtful for a moment. "Not really, no. All I could do for him, really, was to help him get in touch with some key personnel in the lost luggage department. One of the higher-ups."

"Did he ask you about the passengers at all?"

She rubbed at her hair, as if testing whether it was still damp from the shower. "No. Well, he did ask if I remembered the man who was missing his luggage. I can't recall his name at the moment, and I guess it wasn't really luggage, some sort of robot's head or something."

"David Hanson," He said.

"Yes, that was the passenger's name. I remember now."

"So, you do remember him?" He opened his pocket-sized notebook.

"Not really. The only reason the name is familiar is because the other detective asked about him. But the man himself – I mean, he was just another passenger. I don't even remember what he looked like."

He briefly glanced toward Richard. The boy seemed to have tuned out their conversation.

"Did the detective – Poulson – ask about the other passengers?"

"No. I guess he didn't think it was important."

"Then let me ask," he said. "Do you recall any of the other passengers at all?"

She shifted her stewardess cap from one hand to the other, worrying its brim as if fingering prayer beads. "It doesn't work like that. I mean, think how many flights I have. How many passengers. I smile and hand them their drinks. Unless they strike up an unusual conversation or cause an incident, it's all pretty much a blur after a while. They're all kind of anonymous. Or if there's someone famous on the flight, I'll remember that. Richard Gere, once. Oh, and Jack Nicholson caused a stir on one of my flights. He seemed just as loony in person as on screen. He irritated me, but he made me laugh, too."

It was best not to be too easily frustrated. He revised the question. "So, you don't remember any unusual passengers on that particular flight?"

She shook her head.

"Any unusual events or problems during the flight? Unexpected turbulence, or coffee spilled in a passenger's lap? . . . Anything?" He had once been on an international flight when a spilled tray of scalding-hot coffee burned one of the passengers.

She frowned. "Yes. A flight change for some of the passengers . . . that's probably what caused David Hanson to lose his luggage."

"Do any other incidents stand out in your mind?"

"I'm sorry," she said, seeming genuinely concerned. "That was . . . what, it must have been at least seven or eight months ago . . ."

"Only six. And someone must have asked you about the missing luggage soon afterwards." He let her think about that for a moment.

"What about the passenger manifest," he pressed on. "Is there any way you could get hold of it for me? I have the date and flight number. It might help me to speak with some of the others who were onboard."

"I might be able to. I have a friend in Data Processing."

Once more he glanced over at Richard. The boy moved his hands oddly, as if touching something not really there – like a mime, convincing his audience to imagine an object. Brad wondered whether any of their recent words had registered with the child.

"I'd be willing to pay for a copy – call it a finder's fee – say five hundred dollars."

"That's very generous, but I'm really willing to help if I can. It's just that we normally don't give out that kind of information. But I'll definitely do my best."

"Let me give you my card. There's a fax number on it. I'd like to get the information as soon as possible."

"It might take me a few days. Maybe even a week. . ." She seemed to reconsider as they spoke, realizing she might have difficulty actually obtaining the manifest.

"As soon as possible," he repeated. "To be honest, I don't really have any other leads right now, so I'd really appreciate your help."

"You make it sound urgent. All right. I'll try to reach Jill by phone before I drive Richard home. She's the friend I mentioned, in Data Processing."

He tried to think of further questions. Failed. "I won't take up any more of your time, Ms. Nicholson."

"I'll see you out. You've been so nice. I really wish I could be more helpful."

Leaving, he nearly forgot about Richard, but then called "Good-bye" over his shoulder. The child seemed oblivious. Stevie Nicholson surprised him, accompanying him not only to the security gate but beyond, out to his parked rental car. Keys in hand, he hesitated, sensing that she wanted to say something further.

"I wanted to thank you for getting Richard talking like that. He responded to you really well. So often he just sits there without taking any interest in his surroundings. He's not very good at interacting with people." She stood with arms folded against the overcast chill.

"He's very intelligent," Brad said. "It was a strange conversation, but I enjoyed it. Thanks for your help, Stevie. I'll look forward to hearing from you."

Just as he completed backing out from the parking space, a tap sounded on the passenger side window. He hit the window switch.

She took a step closer, resting her folded arms on the car window ledge and leaning her head part way in. "Maybe there was something out of the ordinary that day," she said. "If it was the same flight. I think it might have been. There was this fortyish man on board. He was entertaining several other passengers, doing magic tricks and throwing his voice. I think he was wearing just a little mascara. He asked for a volunteer and a woman a couple of rows over raised her hand. I remember thinking at the time that he probably knew her . . . maybe they were just pretending to travel separately."

"Do you recall if either of them spoke with David Hansen?"

"I really can't say, since I don't remember him that well. For all I know, one of them could have been seated right next to him"

"Get me that passenger list, Stevie. Push it for me." He felt they had established enough rapport to say this. And knew most likely he would never have received this information in a phone interview; his presence, his friendliness, and his involvement with Richard had impressed her. "If you get a chance, call me tomorrow and let me know if you've made any progress."

* * * * *

After the return flight, back in L.A., he located a book shop that specialized in science fiction. A maze of shelves displayed the spines of new and used paperbacks. Off to one side there was a hardbound section, but his budget favored the used books. There was also a section for collectors, with plastic-wrapped copies of books signed by the author; he moved on. Always a quick shopper, five minutes later he carried his harvest of novels to the register: *We can Build You, VALIS, The Three Stigmata of Palmer Eldritch, The Galactic Pot Healer, The Martian Time-Slip, A Maze of Death,* and *The Transmigration of Timothy Archer* – all by Philip K. Dick.

Long haired and fortyish, looking like a hold-over from the psychedelic sixties, the man behind the register informed Brad he was the owner of the bookstore.

Obviously, you like Philip K. Dick," the man asked.

"I've only read three of his books so far, but they were so . . . disturbing? Intriguing? . . . I wanted to see if his other books are as thought-provoking."

"Be careful," the proprietor said. "You'll become an addict. We call them Dick-heads." He grinned when he said it. "Just kidding," he added. It took Brad a moment to figure it out: *Dick-head. As in acid-head or pot-head.*

23

"*We Can Build You*", the proprietor said, thumbing through the stack of books and ringing them up on the register. "I first read it when it appeared as a serial in one of the science fiction magazines. *Amazing Stories*, I think. The title was different for the magazine version. 'A. Lincoln, Simulacrum.'" It was the word his client Isis had used in the office. *A fortuitous connection with the case?* And she had specifically recommended the book, he recalled. He decided to read it next.

"Say," he asked, as the other handed back his credit card; "You wouldn't happen to have a copy of the *I Ching*, would you?" The man behind the register smiled again, and then actually laughed. "Ah, *The Book of Changes*. You've been reading *The Man in the High Castle*, haven't you? I bought a copy right after I read it, too. I'd be glad to loan you my copy, but I don't have it here. Listen, there's an occult book shop just down the street from me. I'm sure they have one there."

And they did. In the New Age of Aquarius Bookstore, a short walk along Santa Monica Blvd., he purchased a copy.

Arriving home, he once more went on a book marathon, up all night reading *We Can Build You* and then getting several chapters into the Palmer Eldritch book. He was loggy-headed when he checked the *Times* for the daily reality index in the morning. It had been hovering in the low-to-mid-eighties the last few days. What had become of the more normal ninety-percent-plus days?

After driving to his office, he thought about researching magicians performing in the Vegas area, but picked up *The Three Stigmata of Palmer Eldritch* again instead. The low reality index had begun to seem appropriate, immersed as he was in such a strange series of books – most likely merely the author's pervasive paranoia seeping into him.

An incoming call rescued him from guilt about not working on the case. "Brandon Andrade's office," he answered, picking up in the middle of the second ring.

"Brad? This is Stevie Nicholson. I've got that list of passengers you wanted. I'll fax it over in a couple of minutes."

"That's great, Stevie. I'll get a check in the mail – really appreciate your help. By the way, did you get a chance to look over the list? Did any of the names look familiar?"

"Yes, I did read through it, just on the off-chance. But Hanson's name was the only one I recognized. There's another reason why I called, though. Richard wanted me to tell you something. When we talked about that android, I didn't think he was listening, but it turns out he was. He says he has a personal computer in 2014, and he's been researching. He says the android wasn't actually built until 2005."

"That's absurd. We both know you were on that flight in late '86 when it disappeared." He paced back and forth on the short leash of the spiraling phone cord, stretching the coils to their limit. The anger in his voice surprised him. "Why are you telling me this nonsense?"

She seemed to hesitate before answering. "Because Richard asked me to mention it. I know it doesn't make any sense, but he seemed . . . concerned. Like he thought it was really important. He made me promise to tell you."

"I'm sorry, Stevie. This case is weird. I guess I'm letting it get to me too much. No reason for me to take it out on you or your nephew."

"That's ok. Sometimes he gets to me, too. He seems so certain about his delusions. Sometimes, you know, he's so consistent, I nearly think they're real. Listen, as soon as we're off the phone, I'll fax you that list. I'm calling from an Office Mack's store."

"That's great, Stevie. Thanks again."

After hanging up he continued pacing. A minute or two later the fax/phone emitted its characteristic coded beeps and began chattering out copy.

He made a number of calls that afternoon between bouts of reading *VALIS*. The letters of the title, he had discovered, were an acronym for Vast Active Living Intelligence System. Each book he read seemed stranger than the last. —And linked, in some elusive way, with his case. Or was that his imagination?

At the pace he was burning through the novels, another trip to the same bookstore might well be in order in another week or two, he decided. There had been a number of additional titles on the shelves.

"You're turning into a Dick-head," he said aloud to himself.

* * * * *

It was, perhaps, an odd hunch. But he liked it.

He had three lists of names. The passenger manifest for flight 302; a list of magicians and ventriloquists who performed in Las Vegas; and a list of similar performers in Dallas. The Vegas list was much longer than the Dallas list, of course.

David Copperfield's name appeared under the Vegas heading. Surely, he was famous enough that Stevie would have either recognized him or known that he was aboard that flight. For the most part he had the list of performers memorized. He worked his way slowly through the names on the passenger manifest, his sense of disappointment increasing as the possibilities dwindled. Finally, his finger froze in place. He had a match – or, at least, a partial match. Minnelli the Magnificent appeared for both Dallas and Las Vegas, and one of the passengers had been named Vittorio Minnelli. It shouldn't be too difficult to find out whether Vittorio Minnelli and Minnelli the Magnificent were one and the same. It was so promising that he said "Yes" out loud and fisted one hand.

A few phone calls later, he discovered that Vittorio, a.k.a. Minnelli the Magnificent, was performing at an off-strip Vegas club and hotel the following weekend. He called the hotel and booked a reservation. He thought about flying, but Vegas wasn't that far away; he decided to drive. And perhaps, on the way back, get in a day or two of off-roading.

He stayed downtown for dinner that night. He was tired on the drive home; too many late nights reading. *Tonight, I'll get some rest.*

Events failed to cooperate. When he entered his apartment, he discovered that it had been ransacked. In his bedroom, drawers had been overturned, their contents spilled. The furniture cushions in the living room had been removed and tossed on the floor. The kitchen cabinets were all open. He did a cursory cleanup, spending nearly an hour setting everything in relative order. As far as he could tell, nothing was missing. What could they have been searching for? In recent days he had been to San Diego and Dallas. Did someone believe, perhaps, that he had located the android head and hidden it in his apartment? *Surely, this isn't that kind of case.* Had the head been in his possession, he would have returned it immediately.

Angered by the invasion of his apartment, the sense of violation, he knew he was too keyed up to sleep. So, he picked up *VALIS,* still unfinished, and read until 2:30 am, finally nodding off in the living-room chair by the lamp.

* * * * *

Dim overhead lights and lamp-oil candles on the tables – he nursed a Bloody Mary and tried to keep anticipation to a minimum. As usual of late, he hadn't slept much the night before, and his head ached. Was he catching a cold? His sinuses were clogged, which always made him feel a little out of touch with the real world, as if his I.Q. had somehow plummeted about 20 points.

The Loose Goose was an off-strip comedy club that also booked offbeat performers like Minnelli the Magnificent. The plush, tuck-and-roll seating appeared mended in a couple of spots, and he wondered if the club would have a shabby look in bright lighting.

The overhead lights dimmed further and then vanished. Only the illumination of the candles remained, making him think of nighttime ceremonies. The patrons grew quiet and someone at another table laughed nervously. They seemed hypnotized and passive, under some sort of somnolent spell, abruptly broken when the bright stage lights burst on. An overweight man in an expensively cut suit and tie stood elevated before them, just in front of the closed curtains.

"Ladies and gentlemen, welcome to the Loose Goose. It looks like we might have a few loose ganders in the audience, too. We've got some great acts for you tonight. Let's start by welcoming Minnelli the Magnificent, the Houdini of ventriloquists!"

The curtains opened in synch with his departure, revealing an ornamented trunk and a stool-like chair occupying the otherwise bare stage.

Vittorio Minnelli entered stage-left, carrying a dummy whose face bore a striking resemblance to the ventriloquist's own. There was no chance whatsoever that this was the android's missing head. The dummy's head with its fixed expression looked wooden. Just as he had quelled his enthusiasm earlier, he now tried to keep his disappointment to a minimum, shaking off the feeling that he had come here on a fool's errand.

"Hey! That stupid emcee didn't introduce me," the dummy seemed to say.

"Calm down, Reggie," the ventriloquist said. "He doesn't think you're real."

"Not real? What does he think I am, a phantom? Doesn't he know I have feelings . . . *hurt* feelings."

"It's all right, Reggie. I'll introduce you. Ladies and gentlemen, this is my nephew Reginald. Please give him a big round of applause."

There had only been a smattering of claps for the ventriloquist. The dummy, though, received an enthusiastic greeting.

Brad knew from his brief researches that the dummy named Reginald was referred to, in performers' jargon, as a "ventriloquial figure".

Minnelli the Magnificent had seated himself on the stool. "Have you noticed, Reggie, that Christmas comes earlier every year?" he said, adjusting the dummy's position on his knee.

"What do you mean?" Reggie asked. "Christmas is always on the twenty-fifth of December."

"Yes," the ventriloquist agreed. "But the decorations in the shops and malls go up earlier and earlier every year. They used to wait 'til after Thanksgiving, but now as soon as Halloween is over you start seeing yule decorations."

"So, what?" Reggie wanted to know. "We're in the middle of summer right now."

"My point is, pretty soon you'll start seeing Christmas trees right after the Fourth of July."

"Wow". The dummy's head swiveled as it looked from the audience to Minnelli. "Then Christmas *must* be getting really close. The Fourth of July is less than a week away. Could we have a virgin Christmas tree this year, Uncle Minnelli?" No smile was painted upon the dummy's face – which reminded as expressionless at that of the ventriloquist.

"What's a virgin Christmas Tree?" Asking the question, Minnelli sounded put-upon, yet patient.

"Why, one that's never been flocked, of course." There were groans from the audience; a few half-hearted laughs. Brad decided the ventriloquist must be desperate for material, telling Christmas jokes this time of the year.

More and more he tuned out the performance, studying the reactions of the audience.

* * * *

Midway through Minnelli's skit, there came a rapping sound, as of someone knocking on a door.

"It sounds like Santini the Sailor is getting claustrophobic," Minnelli said. "Would you like to take a break, Reginald? Maybe a little nap?"

"But I'm not at all sleepy," the dummy said. "Besides, I want to tell some more jokes." Minnelli reached into his trunk and lifted an inflated plastic mini-baseball bat, striking the dummy on its head with his free hand. A drummer somewhere out of sight simultaneously struck his base drum.

Reginald the dummy's eyes crossed and then rolled upward as it said "Now I'm sleepy," a world of weariness in the diminishing tone. Its rolled eyes closed, its form slumped over, and the knocking sound repeated.

The performer placed Reginald in the trunk and drew forth a black box. Reseating himself, he held up the box ceremoniously, as if displaying a work of art. There were symbols or runes painted in gold upon the hinged front or lid, which he opened like a door. Within, there was a face—a head—with a patch over its left eye. It wore a Greek sailor's cap.

"I don't like being kept in the dark," the head said.

Engrossed for the first time since Minnelli began his not-very-hilarious routine, he sat forward until the table's edge pressed hard against his chest. His heart beat fiercely and dark spots throbbed before his eyes, reminding him of how short he was on sleep.

Intent, he studied Sailor Santini's bare chin.

Philip K. Dick's signature beard was missing, but it might have been cut away or shaved. Most likely it had merely been glued in place, and a bit of adhesive remover would solve that problem. Could this be the simulacrum's head in disguise?

It was difficult to tell; the cap and eye patch and naked chin would change the appearance, but still . . .

Lost in thought, he had briefly tuned out the performance. Had there been jokes told on stage? Laughter or applause from the audience? He had a vague impression of the show going on while he was oblivious to the words that had been spoken. But Santini the Sailor's eye blinks, the expressive arching of the eyebrow that was not concealed by the patch – so much like the facial expressions of the android. Only the swiveling of the head from left to right was missing.

"What do you think of Las Vegas," the ventriloquist asked of Sailor Santini.

"I lived in Fullerton once, but I like Las Vegas. I like to play poker and blackjack—"

The non-sequitur immediately caught his attention. Always a thorough researcher, he knew that the author had at one time lived briefly in Fullerton. *This*, he told himself, *is the clincher.* Obviously, Minnelli was letting the head speak for itself, using only its programming. Ideal situation for a ventriloquist; he could relax for a few minutes with no need to speak for the dummy-head. Brads internal gauge hovered near certainty: he had, against odds, solved the case. Now he merely needed to retrieve the stolen property.

Whenever there was applause or laughter, the head in the box shifted its gaze to the audience. He recalled watching the tape of the Dick simulacrum. The eye-movement and varying facial expressions merely offered more confirmation.

"Santini, some of your comments don't sound very intelligent. Why don't you tell the audience what it feels like to be a dummy?"

"I've always been interested in artificial intelligence." This seemed exactly like a comment the Dick android would make.

"Well," Minnelli responded, "You might be artificial, but you certainly aren't intelligent."

"I like talking with *you*," Santini said.

"Folks," Minnelli said, "I'd like to tell you a little bit about our history. Shortly after Santini and I met, back when he had his own sailboat and a parrot named Polly, we struck up a lucrative bargain. We would take passengers out on harbor cruises, and I would entertain them with my dummy Reggie and some magic tricks, making things disappear. But that parrot was so unbelievably annoying. For instance, if I was doing a card trick and made the Jack of Spades disappear, the parrot would say 'It's up his sleeve! It's up his sleeve.' Or let's say I was palming a marble, making the subject or mark choose which hand it was in, the parrot would say 'It's in his left hand, it's in his left hand.'"

Each time Minnelli supposedly quoted the bird's words, he imitated the squawking talk of a parrot.

"And so it went," Minnelli continued. "No matter where I hid something, in my mouth, say, or even my trouser leg, that damn parrot would give it away, ruining my act.

"Then one day, we had the misfortune of striking some rocks, and the sailboat sank. Santini and I managed to save ourselves, holding onto a barrel that was afloat. It turned out that Polly the Parrot had also escaped the wreckage, and I spotted him flying in circles where the boat had vanished. Next thing you know, he flew over to us, landing right atop the barrel. And do you know what that effing bird said to me?"

"What did the bird say?" Santini asked. "This is interesting."

"Don't you remember? It asked me, 'Where did you hide the sailboat?'"

No matter how good a ventriloquist is at bouncing from one voice to another, he cannot speak in two voices at once. But while Santini was saying "This in interesting," Minnelli had interrupted too soon, and for just an instant both voices could be heard simultaneously. The audience did not seem to notice, but Brad certainly had.

Minnelli, meanwhile, was still riffing on the parrot. "I appeal to all of you in the audience, and I'm sure you can understand what I did next. I made that demonic bird disappear. Well, I didn't really make it disappear; I changed it . . .

"I'm familiar with *The Book of Changes*," Santini said. "I made use of it when I was writing —" And the head stopped in midsentence, its face suddenly slack, as if a switch had been turned off.

Minnelli looked angry. "Santini, you do go on too long sometimes, don't you? And all those silly letters you keep writing to your aunt!" But Brad knew the android had been about to mention *The Man in the High Castle*. Obviously, the head had been partially – but not completely – reprogrammed, so that it could take part in the comedy routines. A rechargeable battery compartment must also be built into the custom box; he could not see any cords.

"Anyway, I didn't really make the parrot disappear. I changed it into a polygon." This said with a pause in the middle that made it "polly-gone." But not a single laugh from the audience. *Not that the joke deserved it,* Brad thought.

The momentarily dead-looking android head came back to life.

"All right, Santini, is it time to shut the box?"

"Yes. I need some rest," Santini said. "Besides, we've used up all the jokes we rehearsed. Shut the box."

Minnelli did, and the audience responded with more enthusiasm than Brad would have expected.

The performer returned the box to the same trunk that held his other dummy and props. He gave a deep bow and waited until the clapping mostly faded. "Ladies and gentlemen, there will be a brief intermission. Afterwards, the world-renowned comedic impressionist Pete Jeter will be here to entertain you."

Brad sipped the last of his drink. *So world-renowned that I've never heard of him.*

* * * * *

Time to take action.

He immediately pushed to his feet and started for the hallway to the right of the stage, ignoring the approaching waitress. Earlier he had explored the hallway on the left – only the restrooms and the locked door of a storage or supply room. The offices and dressing room had to be in this direction.

One of the other servers intervened, moving to stand in his way. "Can I help you, sir?" she asked.

"I wanted to see Minnelli the Magnificent backstage. I'm a big fan of his, and I'd really like to get his autograph."

"Sir, I'll need to get the manager's permission —" she began; but he was already pushing past her. He smiled back over his shoulder. "Minnelli won't mind," he said.

Unfortunately, the manager chose that moment to emerge from the office, dapper in his suit and tie. It was the same man who had introduced Minnelli to the audience at the beginning of the show. "I'm sorry, Sir," he said. "We don't usually allow our customers back here." He smiled affably. "How can I help you?"

Brad repeated his request for Minnelli's autograph.

"I tell you what. If he says it's o.k., I'll take you back to see him." The other walked past the office entrance to the door beyond – what must be the dressing room. The manager stepped only partly inside, his head out of sight, evidently looking around. Turning a moment later, he said, "I can't believe it. Minnelli's not in there. And he just finished his show. It's like he disappeared."

Could the performer have been aware of Brad's presence and purpose? *Nearly impossible.*

"Let me check out back," the manager said.

There was a turn at the end of the hallway. The manager followed it. Brad wanted to follow it too, but decided it was best to hold his ground. Returning, the other wore a frown. "His car's not in the parking lot. Usually he hangs around a while after he performs. He must have been in a hurry. . . Minnelli's good about signing autographs, though, so I'm sure he won't mind if I give you his card. Hang on a minute, I've got some in the office."

He wondered whether Minnelli's trunk might still be on the premises, with the android's head inside. Yet he could think of no reasonable way to attain access, even if Minnelli had left it behind.

The Manager stepped through the door marked OFFICE and reappeared a moment later. "Minnelli has a shop here in Vegas," he said. "The address is on the card."

Brad accepted the card and studied it for a moment:

VITTORIO MINNELLI
"MINNELLI THE MAGNIFICENT
MAGIC SUPPLIES & VENTRILOQUIAL FIGURES

With a Saguaro Springs Blvd. address in Vegas.

"Thanks so much." Forcing himself to remain friendly despite his disappointment and frustration, he turned to the waitress. "I guess I will have that other Bloody Mary now."

* * * * *

Late Monday morning, after two cups of coffee laced pale with half-and-half, and after forcing down a breakfast platter of eggs, sausage, and hash browns, he finally managed a semblance of consciousness. His stomach felt uncertain and his head throbbed as if with a hangover, even though he had only consumed the two-drink minimum at the club. Clear thinking was not an option, and the reason was obvious: once more he had stayed up most of the night, this time reading *The Galactic Pot-Healer.* It was the first of the author's books that had struck him as outright hilarious. Several times during the night he had laughed out loud.

Why am I doing this to myself? he wondered. Evidently some ungoverned part of him wanted to absorb every novel Philip K. Dick had ever written.

Shoving his plates aside, he spread a map of Las Vegas atop the casino coffee shop table. Checking the index of street names, he failed to find Saguaro Springs Blvd. Was it, perhaps, a new street, not yet on the map?

He billed the breakfast to his room. A trio of limo-cabs waited in the semi-circular drive fronting the hotel.

He struck up a conversation with several uniformed drivers, but all three denied knowledge of the whereabouts of a street with the name he sought. Baffled for a moment, he slid out his wallet and removed the business card the Loose Goose manager had handed him, verifying that he had given the drivers the correct street name. On impulse he turned the card over; there was a tiny map on the reverse side.

So much for his brilliant powers of detection; he chided himself for not noticing the inked lines before now.

"Oh, wait," he said. "Here it is." He handed it to the nearest uniformed driver, who studied the map on the card.

"Sure," the other said. "I can find this. It's way off the strip, but no problem." On one hand it would be nice to have his wheels with him. But traffic and parking could be such a hassle in Vegas . . . and he did not know where any of the out-of-the-way streets listed on the map were located. He envisioned a series of wrong turns.

Still holding the card, the driver said "Hop in," at the same time opening the cab's door.

And what if he decided to do some illicit locksmithing, jimmying his way into the shop? He did not want his Wrangler parked nearby; it was too easily identified. *Just do it*, he decided, and climbed into the cab.

Navigating by the directions on the business card, the taxi driver passed beneath the I-15 Freeway. Several long blocks and a series of bewildering turns later, he found himself in a part of the city that totally contradicted the glitz and glamour of the strip. Rundown shops lined the street – bail bondsmen and grimy-looking pawn shops. One final turn took them onto Saguaro Springs. It was half a block long, much more of an avenue than a boulevard, terminating in a low metal barrier with desert sands beyond.

After retrieving the card, he paid and tipped the driver. As the taxi pulled away he was struck by a sense of desolation. Aside from what was either a bundled mound of clothing or a transient asleep on the steps of a corner store, the street was empty. Partly because of the lack of traffic—vehicle or pedestrian—the neighborhood had an abandoned look. There were barred display windows all along Saguaro Springs, and the shops were as faded and colorless as the transient's bulky layered clothing, as if the structures had been scoured by wind-blown desert sands. He shook off the feeling that he had arrived at some phantasmal periphery of Las Vegas that existed only on the ventriloquist's miniature map on the back side of a business card. A distant, elevated curve of the I-15 with cars streaming across the overpass was somehow reassuring, an artery keeping him connected to reality.

With hands cupped around his face for a better glimpse of the dim interior, he pressed against the window of the magic shop. A Charlie McCarthy look-alike dummy, complete with top-hat and monocle, stared back at him from the lap of a mannequin meant to represent Edgar Bergen. The sign in the window read CLOSED. He considered picking one of the locks, thinking the back entrance might give more concealment, but when he jiggled and turned the knob, the door swung open, not locked at all.

A distant bell tinkled as he entered Minnelli's shop. The interior was dim, the only illumination the angled spill of sunlight through the windows.

Eerie, all those dangling ventriloquial figures with painted expressions and blind eyes staring at him. *Like walking through a wax museum at midnight*, he decided. He glanced up and around at wall-mounted dummies, some of them not far from the ceiling: rouged cheeks and arching painted brows, many of them with lips lipstick-red – and such a variety of appearances and expressions, from bland fixed eyes to immense, artificial smiles. One of the dummies appeared to focus upon him with cold hilarity, its eyes gleaming. He met its gaze . . . *the smile of a plastic psychopath.*

Where is Minnelli? he wondered. Or, at least, a shop assistant.

As he stepped past a rotating display of small, singly packaged magic tricks and novelty gags, a voice said "How are you, handsome?" The voice, coming from above, startled him. He glanced up at a wire-dangled buxom female dummy in a low-cut cloth dress – obviously, she was rigged with a motion sensor and a recording.

"Hello!" he called out. "Is anyone here?"

Some of the wall mounted figures had plaques below, naming the ventriloquist who had once owned them and sporting outrageous prices, some marked NOT FOR SALE. Evidently this was partly a ventriloquial museum as well as a shop. Some of the older dummies were probably fashioned from papier-mâché; and judging by the grooves on several of the faces, their mouths opened and closed like a nutcracker's.

The counter near the cash register, its upper half encased in glass, held an array of magic tricks and impractical practical jokes in larger packages, more elaborate – and more expensive – than those on the rotating display, including large boxed magic sets. He was still surveying the contents of the case when the lights came on, startling him, and Minnelli approached from a door at the rear of the shop.

"How can I help you?"

"Hi. I'm a big fan of yours. I watched your performance last night. I wanted to see you after the show and ask for your autograph, but you were already gone. The club manager was nice enough to give me your card."

Bereft of makeup and with his stage persona set aside, the ventriloquist seemed a different person. Gone, too, was the phony Italian accent. Vittorio Minnelli was now more relaxed and ordinary looking, and older than Brad had imagined—perhaps in his late fifties.

"Are you interested in ventriloquism?"

"Very interested," he lied. "But strictly from an amateur standpoint. I practice a lot at home, learning to throw my voice . . . but I don't have a dummy . . . yet."

Minnelli shifted gears, suddenly an intent salesman. "I have an excellent collection of ventriloquial figures." He gestured at the walls, where not many bare spaces remained. "Antiques and replicas, as well as originals. If these are out

41

of your price range, I also have some more basic models, a bit crude but excellent for someone developing his skills. . . You say you've been practicing?"

"Well . . . never with an audience. I've never been on stage. Just, you know, standing in front of a mirror and trying not to move my mouth or lips while I talk."

The other led him over near the rear margin of the shop and pointed to a low-mounted dummy with its eye-level nearly identical to their own. It was simpler than the others, with painted eyes that could not blink.

"This is just a basic, commercial model. Nothing original about it." Minelli preened his curled moustache. "Mass produced . . . available pretty much all over the U.S."

He noticed there was no price tag, and assumed, even though there was nothing special about it, the figure would likely be expensive. Another thing he noticed: a layer of dust atop the dummy's head. There was a pervading seediness in the shop, and Minnelli himself seemed to partake of it. The performer wore the same jacket as the night before, now badly rumpled.

"Have you read up on the subject at all? Do you have any textbooks or books of instruction? I have a number of them here in stock. *How to Become a Ventriloquist* by Edgar Bergen is one of the most popular; but I also have other, more scholarly works that you might find of interest."

Time to change the subject, while still allowing Minnelli to think of him as a customer. "I don't see anything like it here, but I've got to say I was really taken by Santini the Sailor. Do you have others like him? Or is he maybe for sale?"

The ventriloquist turned away from him, and when the other spoke again the tone seemed distant and flat. "I don't keep my performance figures here in the shop, and they're not for sale."

"That's a shame. I'd really like to see him up close, though. Maybe after your next performance?"

When Minnelli turned to face him, the entertainer's expression had changed dramatically, shifting to what struck him as a kind of effeminate ferocity. "You're not a fan of mine at all, are you? Who are you, really? And what do you want? Why are you so damn interested in Santini?"

Had he overplayed his role? Sounded too enthusiastic? Even though he had quit LAPD more than five years ago, he knew that he still possessed a cop's aura; had Minnelli read his true demeanor, despite his attempt to conceal it?

"All right," he finally said, opting for honesty. He unfolded his wallet and held it out, showing his P.I. license. It was only good in California, but it was unlikely Minnelli would know this.

"I'm Brandon Andrade, a licensed private investigator. You know why I'm here." Minnelli studied the license briefly and gave a wave of dismissal. "No, I don't know anything. Why don't you tell me?"

"Don't play games. I'm talking about your boxed sailor head."

"I acquired it legally. I have a bill of sale. There's no way you can prove any wrongdoing."

"Yes, I'd like to see that so-called bill of sale. Why don't you show it to me? You created Santini the Sailor from an android's head that disappeared after an airline flight. You disguised the original and reprogrammed it to say the name Santini. It doesn't matter how you acquired it, it's not legally yours. I can have you arrested for possession of stolen property. And keep in mind I can prove you were on that same flight when it stopped in Las Vegas."

"And what if I tell you I still don't know what you're talking about?" Minnelli was just going through the motions, now; his heart wasn't really in it.

"Let's do this the easy way, Minnelli. I can offer you a $1,000 reward for returning lost property. Otherwise we're talking felony theft. The android's head was constructed using state-of-the-art technology. I have a close contact on the Las Vegas P.D." A slight exaggeration. "Do you really want to be arrested? And suffer all the bad publicity that would result? I don't need to mention it would probably screw your career as Minnelli the Not-So-Magnificent."

The other was silent for a moment. "Make it two thousand and I might be persuaded to cooperate."

"No deal. I tell you what, twelve-fifty, and that's my limit. And I'm only willing to offer you that because it will make things easier for both of us." He hated the idea of splitting the reward with Minnelli. But if he didn't negotiate it could make things very difficult. The ventriloquist could deliberately "lose" the head, and it would be impossible to prove the boxed dummy was actually part of the Philip K. Dick android.

"All right; it's a deal. But like I said, I don't keep Santini at the shop. Come in here tomorrow morning at the same time and we'll make the exchange."

"Let's get it now, Minnelli. I don't want you to do a runner."

"Why would I run? I've got shows to do next week. One is at the same club. And you know where my shop is. I can't hide from you."

"*Now*, Minnelli. Forgive me, but I don't trust you." His irony expressed with a fierce tone.

"You don't have an option. If we don't do this my way, I can see to it that Santini does a disappearing act, and no one will ever see him again."

He took hold of Minnelli's left arm, squeezing the man's pliant bicep. "I don't have an option? Wrong. You don't have a choice. We're going together now, to get the android's head." He was tempted to hit the performer but held himself in check.

"All right, all right," Minnelli said. "You win. We'll go now. But please let go of me."

Brad released his grip and the other staggered back a step.

"I've got a gun," a gruff voice called from the opposite side of the room.

Seeming startled, Minnelli turned toward the sound of the voice, and Brad instinctively did the same. No one was there, and when he turned back to face Minnelli, the performer was removing a gun from his coat pocket.

"I really do have gun," Minnelli said, this time in his normal voice. He aimed it casually at Brad, who fumed at the thought of how he had been tricked.

"What next?" Brad asked. He wasn't licensed to carry a weapon in Nevada; only in California. His Chief's Special, freshly cleaned and oiled, was safely under lock and key, back in L.A.

He hadn't figured this was *that* kind of case. A missing android head, for Christ's sake. Since becoming a private detective, he had not once needed to unholster his revolver. Most of his cases had to do with either infidelity or low-level stupidity. Perhaps he had grown too lax. *Maybe,* he thought, *my ransacked apartment should have been a warning.*

"You have no idea what's really going on, do you? I can't begin to explain; there's too much I don't know myself. But there is one thing I'll tell you; I suffer from the time-honored Vegas obsession with wagering. I owe some people some money. I have a meeting this afternoon, and I'm making a down-payment; I can't afford to miss it, or mess around with you, and put my . . . health at risk. But I will meet you here. Tomorrow. Nine a.m. I need the twelve-fifty. I need more than that, but it will help me put together my next payment. In fact, why don't you give me that reward money right now?"

"I don't have it with me."

Minnelli studied him for a moment. "Unfortunately – or fortunately for you, I believe you. All right. Now I'm going to walk you out to your car, and you're going to drive away. Don't try to double back and follow me when I leave."

Brad glared at the performer. "No need to walk me to my car. I'll leave. But I'll have to call a cab. I had one drop me off earlier."

Minnelli grinned. "Forgive me, but I don't trust you." His own words, deliberately echoed, but without the bullying tone. Minnelli gestured with the gun, and followed Brad out the door, looking up and down the street. There were no parked cars. Brad knew the other thought he had lied.

Since the street was empty, Brad figured there had to be a lot behind the shop, where Minnelli had parked.

The ventriloquist gestured with his weapon. "Start walking. If you want Santini, be here tomorrow at nine, like I said."

As he walked, Brad kept glancing over his shoulder. Minnelli just stood there watching until he rounded a corner. What he needed right now was a payphone, to call for a taxi. There had to be one nearby.

Like hell, tomorrow at nine a.m., he thought. *I've got something else in mind for you, Minnelli.*

* * * * *

Sitting in his motel room, he made call after call – Minnelli's agent, the club manager, the police. He wasn't about to wait until tomorrow; Minnelli was anything but trustworthy. He needed the ventriloquist's home address. *Pay him a surprise visit.* If Minnelli wasn't at home, he would break in and search for the android's head.

Finally, he slammed down the phone, totally frustrated. Even his last resource, Craig Landis, who had worked briefly with L.A.P.D. before transferring to Vegas – the two had been on a couple of after-shift bar-hops together – could only produce the information Brad already possessed, the address and phone number of the shop. Minnelli might as well be living out of the back room on Saguaro Springs, though he had seen no evidence of it – aside from the performer's rumpled coat, which proved nothing.

He had two main thoughts in mind: *solve this damn case and get in some off-roading.* He knew there was a great, out-of-the-way route to Barstow he could take on his way back to L.A.

47

Sleep would elude him, he knew. Frustrated, he contemplated going downstairs to gamble. Instead he picked up Dick's *A Maze of Death.*

* * * * *

At 7:30 am the following morning, armed with coffee and donuts, he parked his Jeep Wrangler at the curb across from the shop and half-a-block down.

He took a bite of a maple-frosted donut. Out of sorts, he gazed at the shop window, watching for Minnelli.

He'd quit cigarettes three years ago, but early this morning he'd bought a pack. He lit one and tapped his foot, sipping 24-hour donut shop coffee. Even heavily dosed with powdered whitener, it tasted as bad as expected. He had arrived way too early just in case Minnelli had something in mind. The row of shops was as deserted as the day before – not even a sleeping transient this morning.

He had fretted his way through the night, cursing himself for not forcing the immediate return of the simulacrum's head when he first confronted Minnelli, gun or no gun.

No, not from his cigarette – he squinted and stared – there was smoke roiling up in the window beside the entrance to Minnelli's shop. He tossed the cigarette, got free of his Wrangler, and ran a frantic diagonal across Saguaro Springs. A haze of smoke surrounded the mannequin and the Charlie McCarthy look alike in the window. He spotted flickers of orange light toward the back of the shop.

No time for picking locks; if this wasn't some sort of trick, Minnelli might be somewhere inside, possibly unconscious. He kicked in the door on the third try. Inside, within the flicker of flames just taking hold and the pall of smoke, the figures lining the walls appeared to move their eyes, expressions shadow-shifting. Holding his breath, he charged full-throttle into the back room, which still confined the fire.

He glanced around for a fire extinguisher; failed to find one. Not that it would do much good, at this point. Between the fire's cracklings, it made a sound like someone hissing and spitting at him.

There was enough light from the fire that he could see the large but cramped space, used mostly as a storeroom, cluttered with stacks of magazines and newspapers, some already teased by orange and yellow tatters of flame. There were a few dummies in here, too, a couple of them laid out on a small work-bench for repairs . . . as well as Santini the Sailor, glaring at him from a low shelf, the door of the ornate box tilted open. Had Minnelli lied to him? Had it been here all along?

Don't try to puzzle it out, the damn building's on fire. He grabbed the android head, closed the box, and ran back to the entrance, setting his prize just outside the door.

But his search for the ventriloquist had been far less than thorough—he felt guilty for rescuing the boxed head first and hurried back inside, shouting out Minnelli's name. Time seemed frozen and yet flames were already licking along the back and side walls toward the left part of the storeroom. Somewhere along the way he had started breathing again, the fumes not only caustic but toxic, making his mind reel, a scent that included burning plastic. "Minnelli," he called out repeatedly. There were several high rows of storage shelves, but no ventriloquist sprawled in between. He must have stumbled, or lost it for a moment, because the next thing he knew he was on all fours, on the floor, leaning over a stack of newspapers. His head throbbed; he remembered an explosion of bright and dark stars intermingling.

Awareness came in vague waves. A photo on the front page of the top newspaper – two skyscrapers, one tower belching smoke, the other impaled by the frozen image of a jetliner. *The World Trade Center.* Despite the smoke and the madness of the moment, somehow, he read the date on the newspaper: September 12th, 2001. *But this is 1987,* a lame little portion of his disintegrating thoughts argued. He coughed again and again, uncontrollably.

Finally, he came to – enough, at least, to realize his danger. His repeated nightmare of being trapped in a fire had come true. Instinct took over. And then he was crawling desperately out of the back room, toward the light of the entrance that appeared to recede as he approached. Furnace heat made his eyes water; pushed him backwards. Once he glanced up through the choking smoke to see dummy-features melting, distorted by the tears from his burning eyes.

He sprawled outside on the concrete sidewalk fronting the shop, gulping for untainted air.

Sirens wailed, rapidly approaching.

He raised one hand to the pain at the back of his head: an obvious lump. Something had struck him. Or someone.

A glimmer of reason made him realize he would be a person of interest here at the scene of the fire. If he had the rescued box containing the dummy in his possession, it would seem more suspicious, and would involve a lot of explaining.

There might still be time to conceal it; no fire truck had yet rounded the corner. But the sirens were close – too close. No time to run the long diagonal to his Wrangler down the block – if he could somehow manage to run. Even climbing to his feet, and taking a stumbling step or two, seemed heroic. He did not want to be spotted fleeing from the fire and arrested.

Two doors down there was an abandoned, empty shop with barred windows. A spacious bricked flowerbed bordered the shop front, nothing in it but dirt and litter and several dead, mummified plants. He scooped loose sandy soil aside and buried the closed box with dirt and litter, hoping not too much would spill inside. He shoved one of the desiccated plants atop it and scooped more dirt, turning just in time to see a fire truck rounding the corner.

* * * * *

The rear doors of the ambulance were both open. He sat at the back of the vehicle, his legs dangling down over the bumper.

He watched scurrying firemen and police. Keystone comedy, but he did not find it at all funny. Hose-driven fountains of water played over the roof of the shop and through the ax-broken windows.

When the first fire truck arrived, he had voiced his concern – the words a croak – that someone might be inside.

They were treating him for smoke inhalation. Per instructions, he held an oxygen mask tight to his face. A tube from the mask trailed backwards into the ambulance. Flashing lights and emergency vehicles were everywhere—three patrol cars, a fire truck, and a fire department ambulance in addition to the commercial ambulance that was treating him.

It was not truly a tailgate that he sat upon, and yet he thought ironically: *There must be better tailgate parties than this one.*

He had a clear view of the planter where he had hidden the android's head. The dead plant had toppled aside, clearly revealing one corner of the ornate box. Not glancing its way repeatedly required an effort of will.

Once more he explored the lump on the back of his head. Had Minnelli struck him from behind? Collect insurance money and get rid of Brad at the same time? It made no sense. Why not collect the money for the android's head first? Why have it in the shop at the time of the fire? Why destroy so many valuable antique dummies?

Perhaps someone else, believing him to be Minnelli, had left him to die in the burning shop.

An L.V.P.D. officer approached. "I need to ask you a few questions."

He lifted the oxygen mask slightly – "Sure, go ahead" – and set it back in place. His words came out slightly muffled. He considered moving the mask aside but decided instead to hold it in place. It functioned as a mask in more ways than one.

"Can you tell me why you were in the vicinity of the fire?"

"I was here to see Vittorio Minnelli, the owner of the shop. I was going to purchase one of his dummies." "Purchase" wasn't the most truthful word, but it suited his needs. "When I saw the fire through the window, I was afraid he might be trapped in there. So, I kicked down the door."

"Could I see your driver's license, Sir?" He produced it per instructions, careful that the officer did not spot his private investigator's license. The officer identified himself as Sergeant Anderson as he carefully wrote down Brad's name and address.

"Did you know this Minnelli very well?"

"No. I first met him yesterday, although I did see one of his club performances Sunday night."

"You came all the way from L.A. to see him and buy a . . . dummy?"

"Not really. I came for the gambling, too." Now he was into telling outright lies.

He still felt light headed. The questioning went on and on, and he wasn't sure how long he could maintain his façade. He deliberately failed to mention the blow to his head. Despite himself, he glanced at the box in the planter more than once.

When the officer seemed satisfied, Brad said "I need to be back in L.A. tomorrow, if possible. Or do you need me to stay in Vegas?"

"I don't think so. We know how to reach you. You're free to go. But I'd recommend you get checked out at the hospital first."

Once the officer drifted away, he was confronted by the ambulance driver. "We really do need to get you to the hospital."

"No, that's not necessary. I'm fine," he lied.

The driver, in his white uniform, launched into a lecture. "Listen to me. Fifty to eighty per cent of the deaths from a fire are caused by smoke inhalation. Sometimes the worst of the symptoms are delayed for as much as forty-eight hours. Come on, let's drive you over to Desert Springs Hospital; get you a thorough checkup."

"I told you I'm fine. If I have any complications I'll come in."

"You're saying you want to sign a refusal form?"

"Yes," he answered.

"All right, then." Voice hostile, the other angrily thumped the clip boarded form. "But I'm making a note it's against my recommendations."

Soon, he thought, *I'll be free.*

* * * * *

He waited until 3:00 am to return for the android's head. He had been leery of the evening hours; what if some fire department inspector worked late, seeking evidence of arson? It seemed unlikely, but he had no idea of their hours, and he did not wish to run into anyone else either, so waiting until the wee hours of the morning seemed best.

He kept a few Benzedrine tablets for emergencies. Although he seldom used them, he popped a couple of the bennies now to stay alert, washing them down with swallows from another cup of donut-shop coffee, this time black and way too acidic. The author's famed misuse of pills came to mind. *Just because you're a Dickhead,* he told himself, *don't turn into a pill-head too.*

He turned onto Saguaro Springs. By now he was familiar enough with the turns that he did not need to consult the map on the back of the card.

The neighborhood was deserted; almost dream-like.

After the debacle of the fire, there had been plenty of free time. Too much free time. He had stayed in his hotel room, reading Philip Dick's final novel, *The Transmigration of Timothy Archer.*

54

He was well past halfway through the book when his headache closed in, a tightening vice, and he started coughing again . . . evidence that he should have allowed himself to be transported to the hospital for further treatment and tests.

Ironic that he had been treated for smoke inhalation the same day he started in on cigarettes again. No desire to light one now; his lungs still felt scalded. Besides, he had tossed the nearly full pack of Pall Malls into a hotel-room trash basket.

Afterwards, he had phoned his own office and punched in the code for remotely checking messages: one from Isis, responding to his most recent progress report, and one from the stewardess.

"I'm sorry to bother you again, but Richard insisted I call. He says that his future self has been doing research on something he calls 'the internet'. He says that the original head of the android was never located; a new one, a substitute, even better than the first, was built in 2010. He's worried, and he says you need to be extra-careful. He says you should quit the case.

"I know you don't want to hear all this," she continued. "And I know it's nonsense. But Richard is so convincing, he's got me worried about you, too. Please call me and let me know that everything is o.k."

Well, maybe he would call Stevie Nicholson once the case was closed. Maybe he would even ask her out, despite the inconvenience of a long-distance relationship.

The only positive: somehow, he had managed seven hours of uninterrupted sleep. And when he finally woke, his throat and chest felt better.

A surge of adrenalin ran through him as he pulled up in front of the shop with the brick planters. All through the previous evening he had pushed away his fear that someone would discover the box; that it would no longer be there. But the corner still protruded. He dug the box out and blew off loose dirt. When he opened the small door, everything inside looked fine.

The street was darker than expected. There were several streetlights, but only the one on the corner appeared to be working. Las Vegas was a city of lights; this dark neighborhood, in contrast, was unreal. He placed the android's head in his Wrangler and drove away, expecting a sense of relief: *Case closed.*

Instead he felt paranoid, glancing again and again into his rearview mirror.

* * * * *

The air conditioner labored; sunlight and heat from the Mojave Desert forced their way into the Wrangler like invisible forces expanding. The ascending road became a washboard surface, torturing the jeep's suspension and vibrating him mercilessly. He slowed; slowed again. He was less and less certain about dirt-roading his way to Barstow. Why drive into the open desert when he could have already arrived back in L.A., completing his assignment? *Collecting my fee; claiming my reward.*

Starting with US 95, he had taken a series of highways south from Las Vegas, dropping down into Arizona. He stopped briefly in Fort Mohave, where he connected with the old Mojave Road or Trail – one hundred forty miles of unmaintained dirt road over rough terrain. His chosen route to Barstow. And he knew, really, why he had come this way. To clear his head. To celebrate solving this crazy case.

"Hi, I'm Santini the sailor," the boxed head beside him said, its voice muffled by the closed lid. He had seat-belted the box into the passenger seat . . . Santini riding shotgun, so to speak.

"What's your name?" Perhaps the noisy ride over the hill's washboard road had triggered the head's computer – the sound mistaken for human speech. "Are you there?" it asked.

Amused, he reached out, shifting the box and opening the door. "Sorry if I've been keeping you in the dark."

One of the android's eyes was still covered by the ridiculous-looking patch; Brad could see its visible eye shifting, seeking him out. "It's a common theme in my writing that a dark-haired girl shows up at the door of the protagonist and tells him that his world is delusional."

Jesus. He thought about the brunette Isis, knocking on this door. She had not told him he was delusional, but the VHS tape she had given him, the novels she had encouraged him to read, the case she had hired him to investigate, and the seemingly inevitable events that had followed, including a newspaper pretending to be from the future – all conspired to unsettle him.

The android head continued, "I often write about deranged private worlds." And that made him think about Richard, Stevie's nephew, lost in his individual, isolated, and illogical realm. Or was it suggesting that he had found his way into a deranged private world?

"You haven't told me your name yet."

He glanced toward Santini. "My name is Brad." Why was he playing along? Just shut the damn thing off and shut it up.

"Now that I know your name and what you look like, my facial recognition software will enable me to identify you any time we speak."

"That sounds like a threat." He grinned. Stupid robot.

"Life can often prove threatening, in various ways," the head said. "That's why I believe paranoia is perfectly justifiable. I often feel paranoid. And, I don't quite understand it, of late I feel so . . . disembodied."

"That's almost funny. It sounds like something you would say in one of Minnelli's routines."

Santini shifted its gaze away, and back again. "Minnelli? I know Minnelli. Is he here? I'd like to talk to him, too."

The conversation was beginning to possess its own momentum. He responded as if to a real person. "No. I have no idea where Minnelli is. It seems he's done a vanishing act."

The android's head frowned thoughtfully. "That makes sense, in a way. After all, he is a magician, isn't he? He told me he does magic tricks."

Very clever. It almost sounds like you have a sense of humor."

"You're trying to overinflate my ego, Brad . . . but please, don't stop."

Was that smoke? No, steam, rising from his overheated radiator. *A split in the hose?* He cursed.

"I know you're still there," the head said. "I can see you. Wouldn't you like to have a philosophical discussion?"

"Shut the fuck up."

"I flunked a class once myself," it said. Evidently it was not programmed to recognize the over-used expletive.

He fisted both hands and pounded them against the steering wheel. After climbing out of the jeep he slammed its door hard behind him. Reaching back in, he shut off the ignition, fearing the block might crack if he left the engine running. Fortunately, he had a five-gallon acrylic can of water in the back of the jeep, in addition to five gallons of extra gasoline. And a couple of rolls of electrical tape. Perhaps he could locate the split in the hose and tape it. If he was lucky, the mend would hold the pressure. It was even possible he had a slow leak, and after letting the engine cool for a couple of hours he could add water and be on his way.

The gasoline canister was mounted at the rear, beside the spare tire. He unlocked its hitches and hefted, sloshing it, making sure it was full. After refastening the clamps, he opened the rear compartment of the jeep. *O.K., the water and the tape.*

Except that, standing at the back of the jeep, searching, he could not find the water container. And the damn thing was big enough that it shouldn't take much of a search. A few minutes later, after checking out the entire vehicle, he knew that he could not have overlooked it. He stood there sweating in the intense sunlight, thinking. Remembering. A month or so ago, he had parked the jeep in the garage so that he could clean out the over-cluttered rear of the vehicle, setting the water container to one side, near the wall. His neighbor Valerie had seen the open garage door and entered to talk and, as always, flirt a little with him. How distracted had he been? Was the water container still sitting in his garage? Yet he would swear he had seen it there, in the Jeep, exactly where it was supposed to be, within the past several days.

Self-disgust muted his anger, but only for a moment.

He knew better. Oh, did he know better. He was an Off-Road Reveler, for God's sake. A long-time member, veteran of more than a dozen caravan jaunts through the back country of at least four states of the Union. It was a cardinal rule that off-roaders traveled together. What a fool he had been to come alone, unaccompanied by a parade of helpful redundancy and friends who always had your back. And without double-checking all his supplies.

Tape in hand, he paced beneath the hot floodlight of the sun, allowing the engine another fifteen minutes to cool. Taking off his sweaty shirt, he used it to insulate his hands from the scorching metal, opening the hood. He also used the bunched shirt on the radiator cap, opening it halfway to relieve the pressure first. He could feel scalding heat right through the cloth.

The steam was played out. No boiling water erupted. After removing the radiator cap, he shined a flashlight into the hole, adjusting angles so that he could see down into the darkness. The radiator's chamber looked bone-dry.

A brief exploration revealed the split in the hose. It looked like a cut as much as a split. That pit-stop he had made at Fort Mohave . . . could the damage be sabotage? He mended the hose slowly, with overlapping turns, careful to lay the tape flat and avoid twisting.

Might someone have cut the hose and then taken his water? But he had told no one he was driving into the desert. And if it was all about the android's head, why had it remained safely strapped in place? *Am I being too suspicious? Most likely this is all my doing.*

Surrounding low scrub was useless; the only possible shade was in the jeep. He couldn't afford to run the air conditioner; even if it worked, he would run down the battery. After climbing back inside, he rolled down all the windows, hoping for a breeze. As far as he could tell, the air was completely still.

He had known this dirt-road excursion was risky, but he liked taking risks. Except, in this particular instance, not so much. According to the odometer, he was 45 miles from Fort Mohave. The interstate was probably closer.

This was the second day in a row he had not bought a newspaper or checked the reality index. He knew it had to be low.

Take inventory, he told himself. But the results were far from encouraging. There was only one useful thing he could think of: two cans of cola on the floor of the passenger side, linked together by the plastic thingamajig that held together a six-pack. Except that he didn't have a full six-pack. If he did, he might have been tempted to experiment, and pour it all into the radiator. But he didn't think two cans would be enough to help, and it would leave him with nothing to drink; better to sip them slowly and keep himself hydrated – despite the fact that cola often left him feeling even thirstier. And hadn't he read somewhere that cola, as opposed to hydrating, dehydrated? *It's mostly water,* he argued with himself. *Maybe it will help.*

After nightfall it should be possible to see the lights of some desert town, or distant headlights on the freeway, and set off on foot pursuing them. It was something to hope for. Here, less than fifty yards from the hill's summit, even far-away lights should be easily visible – and if necessary he could hike to the hilltop and check out every horizon. Of course, nightfall was a long way off. Better if he had a way to pass the time, rather than sitting here fretting.

When the time came, he would drive the Wrangler as far as possible. Then, when the engine seized up, he would hike the rest of the way.

Now might be a good time to finish reading *The Transmigration of Timothy Archer*, Philip Dick's final novel; it would keep him from thinking about the corpses of foolish off-roaders found in the desert. He was certain it had happened before in the Mojave. He retrieved the book from the box containing his collection of Dick novels. After thumbing through and locating his place, he fell once more into the narrative.

Feeling shitty, he forced himself to keep reading. Every time his concentration flagged, he peered into the rearview mirror, looking for approaching vehicles or dust-plumes kicked up by motorcycles. Nothing. Nothing at all.

Forty-five minutes later, nearing the end of the book, deep into chapter thirteen, he came to the scene where Bishop Timothy Archer's car breaks down in the desert with two bottles of soda pop inside, and his body is found two days later. He roared out his anger and frustration. The android was his only audience.

He tore the paperback novel in two, ripping along the entire length of the spine, and threw the pieces into the desert.

"Shit!" he shouted. And then shouted it three more times.

The head jittered to life. "Hi, my name is Santini the Sailor", it said. "Oh, it's you, Brad. Just calm down. It's been my experience that most situations in life contain humorous elements."

Hadn't he turned Santini off? He was sure he had.

The fact that the fictional character Timothy Archer had died in the desert in Israel, and he was in the Mojave, provided no comfort at all. *Too damn many coincidences.*

A good conspiracy theory would explain all this. Of course, it would have to include everyone from Isis to Stevie Nicholson, her nephew, and Vittorio Minnelli. And he might as well throw the manager of the Loose Goose and the proprietor of the bookstore into the mix. *And me*, he thought. He was as responsible as anyone else for creating his present dilemma. Yet he was well aware that, like every conspiracy theory he had ever encountered, it would not survive rational analysis.

Maybe, somehow, it was all real. Richard had said the head would never be found. And his present situation explained why it would never be recovered. *Just what I need*, he thought. *A schizophrenic's crazy oracular prophecy.*

Despite feeling light headed, he tried to focus on possible strategies.

Before I try to hike out of here tonight, he thought, *maybe I should bury the damn head here in the desert.* The hell with the reward. Bury it somewhere randomly where no one would ever find it again. Maybe that way he could escape this web of events. Survive his own foolishness.

He could not merely sit here, behind the wheel of the Wrangler, waiting for darkness.

Do something.

There was a backpack in the Wrangler. He could fill it with supplies for his hike.

Standing once more behind the vehicle, he opened a sealed container of trail mix, alternating small handfuls of nuts and raisins with sips of warm cola. He re-sealed the container and placed it in the backpack, along with some energy bars and the one remaining unopened cola can. Rummaging, he added a can of pork and beans and a can opener. He fumbled in vain through the back of his Jeep looking for anything else that might prove useful. His gaze fell on the box containing his Philip K. Dick books. His copy of the *I Ching*, stashed in the same box, suddenly came to mind.

He recalled how, faced with personal problems, the characters in *The Man in the High Castle* had cast *I Ching* hexagrams.

Why don't I cast my own hexagram? he thought. At least it would allow him to take some kind of action while he waited for darkness; another way to pass the time and avoid thinking too much. He did not possess any yarrow stalks, of course, but he knew from reading the book's introduction that he could use coins instead. He had plenty of change in his pocket — change that he might never be able to spend.

He opened the locked flaps of the box and pulled out his *I Ching* – purchased soon after reading *The Man in the High Castle*.

Because he was seriously considering leaving it buried in the Mojave Desert sands, he took the ornamental box containing the android head with him, along with *The Book of Changes*, and – a last-second impulse – the large, festively-colored beach towel with its pattern of frolicking dolphins. Identical to his daughter's. Purchased at Sea World less than two weeks ago. It seemed like another lifetime.

He hiked about thirty yards from the road.

"Where are you taking me, Brad?" the box-muffled voice of Santini said.

"I turned you off, damn you. I know I did."

Spreading the beach towel on the far side of a creosote bush and sat down facing away from the Wrangler. The rules for determining the lines of his hexagram using coins were complicated. He decided to use the three-coin option and reviewed the instructions. This was the first hexagram he had ever cast. He felt obligated to do it precisely, even though he knew divination was nonsense.

Cupping three quarters in joined hands, he jiggled them and tossed them onto the towel, not wanting to lose them in the sand.

Why am I doing this? he wondered. *This isn't like me at all.* It was as if some other personality had invaded him, taking control, forcing him to senselessly cast coins onto a beach towel in the middle of the Mojave. But he continued to toss, again and again, each time counting the heads and tails and writing down the results, solid and broken lines, all the while concentrating on his question: *How do I keep from dying in the desert?* Five minutes later he had his cast. He looked it up in the book: Hexagram 45. It was labeled "Ts'ui / Gathering."

"The lake rises by welcoming and receiving Earth's waters.
"The King approaches his temple.
"It is wise to keep audience with him there.
"Success follows this course.
"Making an offer will seal your good fortune.
"A goal will be realized now."

The expanded interpretation for line 3 caught his attention and seemed promising — or not. *"You strive to find common ground that doesn't exist. Sighing in sadness and walking away would be understood, though you may think less of yourself."*

For a time, he sat there in the ghostly shade of the creosote bush. Staring at the scrawny lines of shadow shaped vaguely like spindly branches and tiny leaves where their image was cast onto the sand, he contemplated the meaning of the hexagram. He felt ill and faint. Did he have a concussion? The back of his head still felt tender; swollen where he had been struck. He imagined a swelling brain, pressing against its skull. His chest was tightening up again; simply breathing in and out seemed difficult. The Mojave heat was unremitting.

Finally, he pushed to his feet. He lifted the towel and the *Book of Changes*. Lifted, too, the boxed head, and carried it with him back toward the Jeep. He limped a little, his foot still bruised from kicking in the door of the shop. *The King approaches his temple.* Well, the Wrangler might well become the android head's temple if Brad didn't get rescued – or manage to rescue himself.

It is wise to keep audience with him there. "Guess I'm going to have another talk with you," he said to the box. And then he added, "What the fuck am I doing?"

Seated in the Wrangler again, he flipped the switch on the base of the box.

"O.K.", he said. "Let's talk."

He slipped off the absurd eye-patch and stared into the unreadable face. The face of Philip K. Dick.

"I like talking to *you*. I like talking about philosophy and religion," the android said. "I'm particularly fascinated by the final, illusive nature of reality."

Making an offer will seal your good fortune. "It looks like I'm going to make you an offer." He stared into the android's eyes and then looked away, studying the random calligraphy of far-away desert ridges.

"Offerings often have a religious connotation," the head said. "Consider this, Brad, from Psalm 50: 'I am God, your God. Not for your sacrifices do I rebuke you; your burnt offerings are continually before me. I will not accept a bull from your house or goats from your folds. For every beast of the forest is mine, the cattle on a thousand hills.'"

"Yes," Brad muttered. "Indeed, they do. Offerings. Have a religious connotation."

The head ignored his words and spoke again. "This is a ritual I do the same every time. I'm great; how about you?"

Brad turned on the driver's seat, facing the boxed head. "I tell you what. This is my offer . . . and no bull. Or goats. I won't bury you in the desert. If I survive, I'll carry you out of here with me. I promise. What do *you* say?"

"Promises are often burdensome or problematical. Still, I try to keep my word, even

67

though everything I say is programmed. But then, everything humans, animals, and robots do is programmed . . . to a degree."

He rubbed at his face. "So, do we have a bargain?"

The android smiled knowingly, in a way that he had never seen it smile before. "I've been waiting for *this* moment for a long time." *So alive, those eyes.* And were some of its comments, perhaps, too discerning?

"Enough of this nonsense," he said. He turned off the switch and closed the box's door so that he would not have to see the face anymore. It became increasingly disconcerting, talking to the thing. Their entire conversation, reverberating in his thoughts, struck a hallucinatory chord.

Checking his watch, he found it was nearing five pm. Still a long time before summer darkness closed in. A nap might have helped, providing a little energy for the long hike to come, but he was too anxious to sleep.

Afterwards, he waited. He sipped more of the warm cola, and strangely enough, gradually began to feel better, even managing to summon a little optimism.

For a while he sat there dozing, never quite managing to fall completely asleep. In immeasurable increments, shadows slowly lengthened. Finally, when he judged the time right, he put the backpack on the front seat with Santini and climbed upslope, walking just to one side of the washboard road.

On the hilltop he turned, surveying all 360 degrees of desert. Nothing, anywhere, moved. Though he had hoped for an evening breeze, the air remained still. The lengthening shadows merged into one.

Even casting the *I Ching* seemed to fit into someone else's plan, merely another aspect of a universe aimed, like a gun, at his head.

How can I break the pattern?

Dusk brought a slight reprieve from the heat, but not much. He still vacillated about burying the box. He kept thinking of Richard's warning that the android head had never been found. Silly to feel obligated by the promise he had made to a rudimentary artificial intelligence. *Still,* he thought, recalling what the android had said, *I like to keep my word.*

He shoved his hands deep into Levi pockets and looked downslope at the Wrangler. It already had an abandoned look. Or was that his imagination?

When I see lights in the distance, I'll know exactly what to do.

Interstate 15 had to be somewhere north of him; but how many miles? Closer than Fort Mohave, certainly. But there was more chance for rescue if he hiked along the dirt road.

He scuffed at twilit dust and turned in a widdershins circle. Lights or no lights to guide him, he would hike his way out of here.

And when I look up and see the stars in their familiar constellations, and the sprawl of the Milky Way, I will finally realize that all of this is real and important, and happening now, within this present moment.

Right now. . . And forever.

CPSIA information can be obtained
at www.ICGtesting.com
Printed in the USA
BVHW041354290421
606136BV00004B/449

9 781087 963846